MY DADDY'S GOT TATTOOS

Story by Andy White
Illustrations by Anita Lester
Design by Emma Byrne

Copyright © 2014 Andy White

First Australian print run.
Limited Edition of 1,000 copies.

ISBN: 978-1-925171-11-2
Published by Vivid Publishing
P.O. Box 948, Fremantle
Western Australia 6959
www.vividpublishing.com.au

Cataloguing-in-publication data is held at the National Library of Australia.

ACKNOWLEDGEMENTS
Paul & Robyn White, Jo Simpson, Nick Reid @ SKUNX Tattoos London, Hal Cheshire @ Tattoos From Hal & Green Lotus Tattoos
Melbourne, Ari Neville, Jason Breward, Paul Nash-Clarke, Tania Jovanovic, Liam Wood, Amanda Beardmore, Kevin Mack & The Rites
Of Passage 2014 Team, VIVID Publishing. All those whose faith in this project has helped keep me going throughout this journey.
Cheers. Feel the love, Andy White

Story and illustrations © 2008-2014 Andy White @ CELEBRITIES ANONYMOUS.

For Toby and Harvey

My Daddy looks different to some other Daddies.

That's because my Daddy's got tattoos.

Some of them are scary, some are crazy, some are big and some of them are small. Some are pictures and some are patterns. Some of them are words or numbers.

Daddy can make one dance when he moves his arm. This makes me laugh because Daddy and me do a little dance at the same time. When Daddy does the dance, he looks like he should be in a circus or a zoo.

When Daddy reads me stories, I pretend that Daddy's tattoos join in the story with the pictures in the book. Sometimes I see Goldie Locks and the Three Bears riding on a dragon's back. Sometimes I see Hansel and Gretel playing with a tiger.

I like looking at all the pictures on Daddy's arms. They are magical. While we are all asleep they come alive and go on adventures. Daddy says that as soon as I fall asleep some of them come into my bedroom to make sure no monsters can ever come to eat me up. I'm glad my Daddy's got tattoos because I don't want to be eaten by monsters.

Auntie Joanna thinks Daddy's tattoos are silly and he should grow up. She does not have any tattoos and Daddy says, "She's just being silly."

Auntie Joanna always says, "No, that's not it at all. Your Daddy will always be my silly older brother who should grow up."

But I love my Daddy just the way he is.

Auntie Jessica also has lots of tattoos. I think she's really nice because she bakes yummy cupcakes. Every time we visit her, she always has a big plate of cupcakes on her kitchen table for us.

Auntie Jessica isn't like Auntie Joanna because she thinks Daddy's tattoos are cool. Auntie Jessica thinks my Daddy should never grow up. Sometimes they both act like children. I think it's funny when they do.

When I was born Daddy got my name tattooed in a love heart. He said he did that because he wants the whole world to know he is going to love me forever.

He did the same when my baby sister was born too.

Sometimes Daddy lets me put on fake tattoos and we play a joke on Grandma. I say to her, "Look Grandma, I've got tattoos. Just like Daddy's."

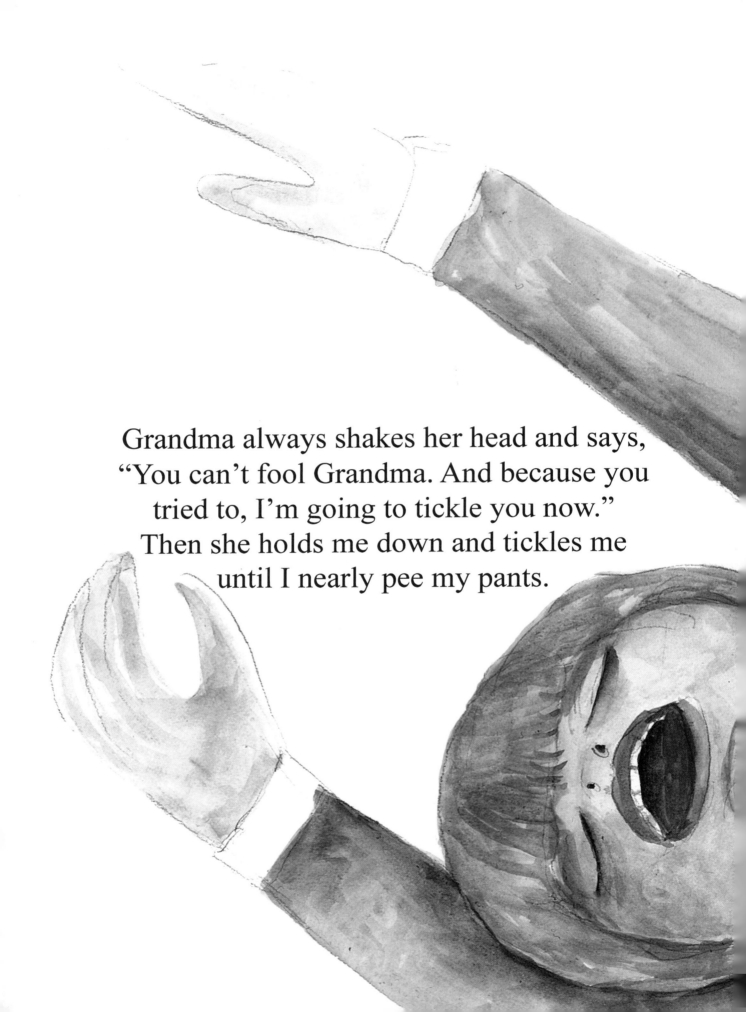

Grandma always shakes her head and says, "You can't fool Grandma. And because you tried to, I'm going to tickle you now." Then she holds me down and tickles me until I nearly pee my pants.

When we go swimming, sometimes people point and stare at Daddy's tattoos.

This makes Daddy smile and say, "It's okay, I don't mind what they say. I know I look funny to some people. But everyone looks funny to someone."

So, I always say to him, "I don't think you look funny Daddy."

"Thank you. That's because you're seriously SUPER DUPER COOL," he says back as he gives me a big hug. Then he lets me jump off his shoulders into the water.

Some people don't like my Daddy's tattoos but I don't care because he's my Daddy.

Every day I tell my Daddy, "I love you and I love your tattoos." Then I give him a big hug.

Every day my Daddy says, "I love my tattoos too but not as much as I love you."

Lightning Source UK Ltd.
Milton Keynes UK
UKIC02n1836040614
232751UK00017B/120